Piece = Part = Portion

Fractions = Decimals = Percents

BY **Scott Gifford**

PHOTOGRAPHS BY **Shmuel Thaler**

TRICYCLE PRESS

Berkeley | Toronto

Hello   Hola   Bonjour

Each of these words mean the same thing—a friendly greeting—in a different language.

Glad   Merry   Joyful

Each of these words refers to the same thing—a happy feeling—in a slightly different way.

Fractions   Decimals   Percents

Each of these words describes the same thing—a part of something—by a different name.

Fractions look like this: $\frac{1}{2}$	and sound like this:	one half
Decimals look like this: .50	and sound like this:	point five zero
Percents look like this: 50%	and sound like this:	fifty percent

The fraction $\frac{1}{2}$ means "1 divided by 2". To find the decimal version of $\frac{1}{2}$, divide 1 by 2 and the result is the decimal .50.

$$\frac{1}{2} = 2\overline{\smash{)}1.00}^{\,.50}$$

To find the percent version of .50, multiply .50 by 100 ("percent" means "for each hundred"), add a percent sign and the result is 50%.

$$.50 \times 100 = 50\%$$

It often seems as though fractions, decimals, and percents are three separate, unconnected ideas. But fractions are used for more than just to show parts of things. Decimals are not only used when working with money. And percents can be used for much more than just calculating sales tax and interest.

In the language of mathematics, fractions, decimals, and percents are three different, but connected, ways of describing the same parts of things.

$\dfrac{1}{2}$ **of a pair of shoes**

.50   50%

$$\frac{1}{12}$$

of a dozen eggs

.08   8%

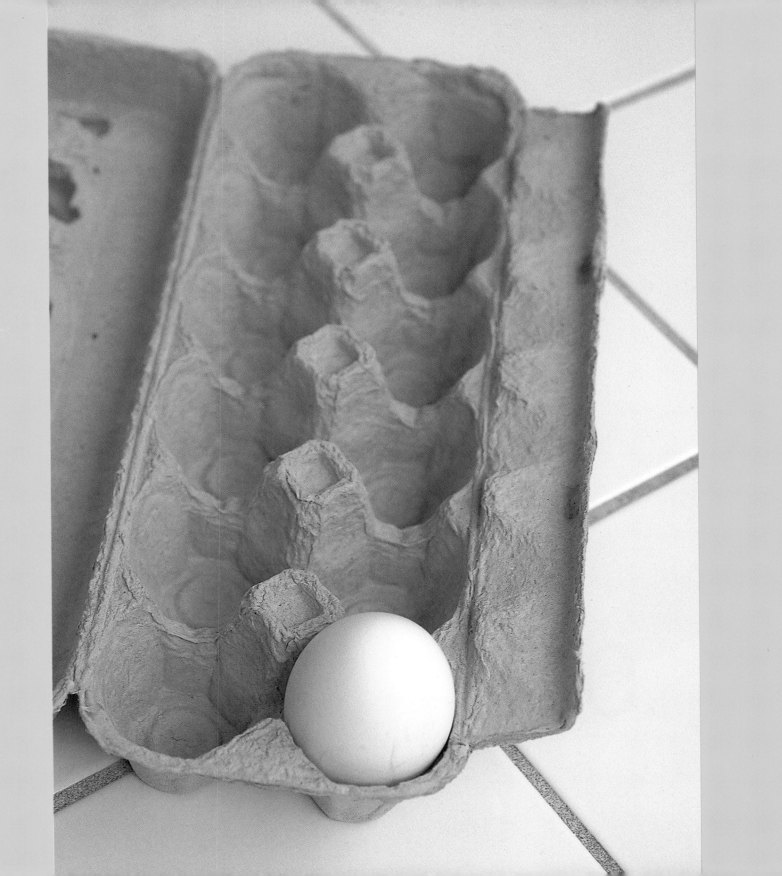

$$\frac{1}{11}$$

of a soccer team

.09

9%

$$\frac{1}{10}$$

of your toes

.10   10%

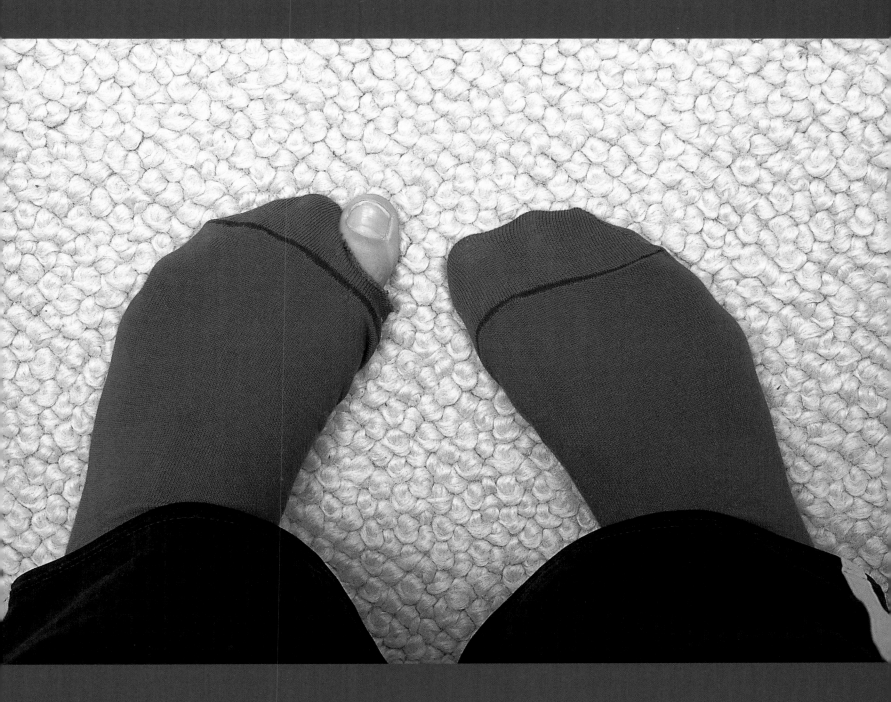

$$\frac{1}{9}$$

of a tic-tac-toe game

.11   11%

$$\frac{1}{8}$$

of a pie

.125   12.5%

$$\frac{1}{7}$$

of a week

.14   14%

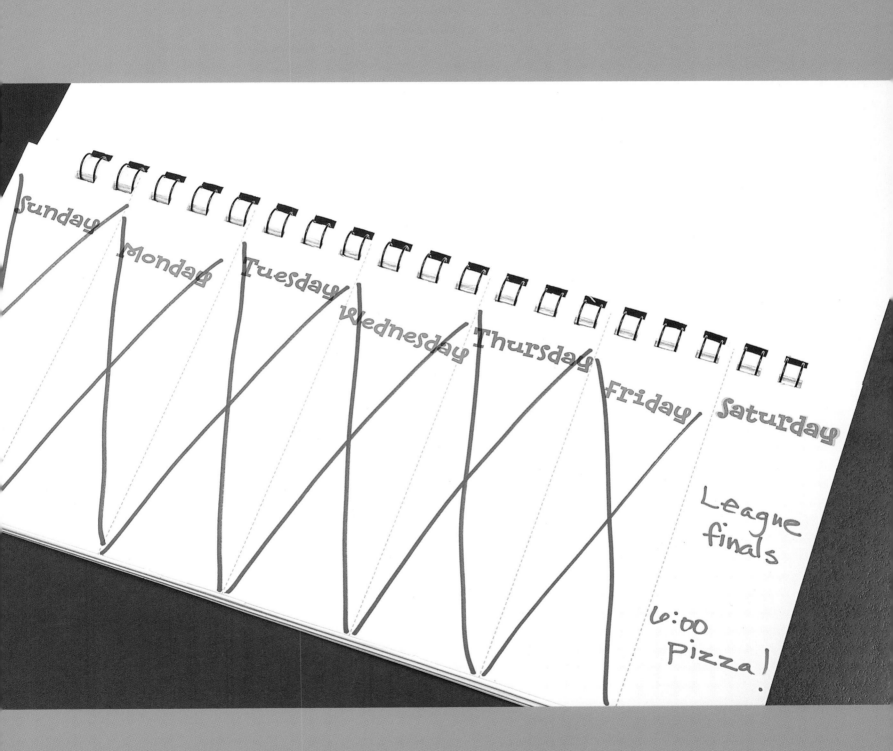

Sunday

Monday

Tuesday

Wednesday

Thursday

Friday

Saturday

League finals

6:00 Pizza!

$$\frac{1}{6}$$

of a six-pack

.166   16.6%

$$\frac{1}{5}$$

of a pack of gum

.20   20%

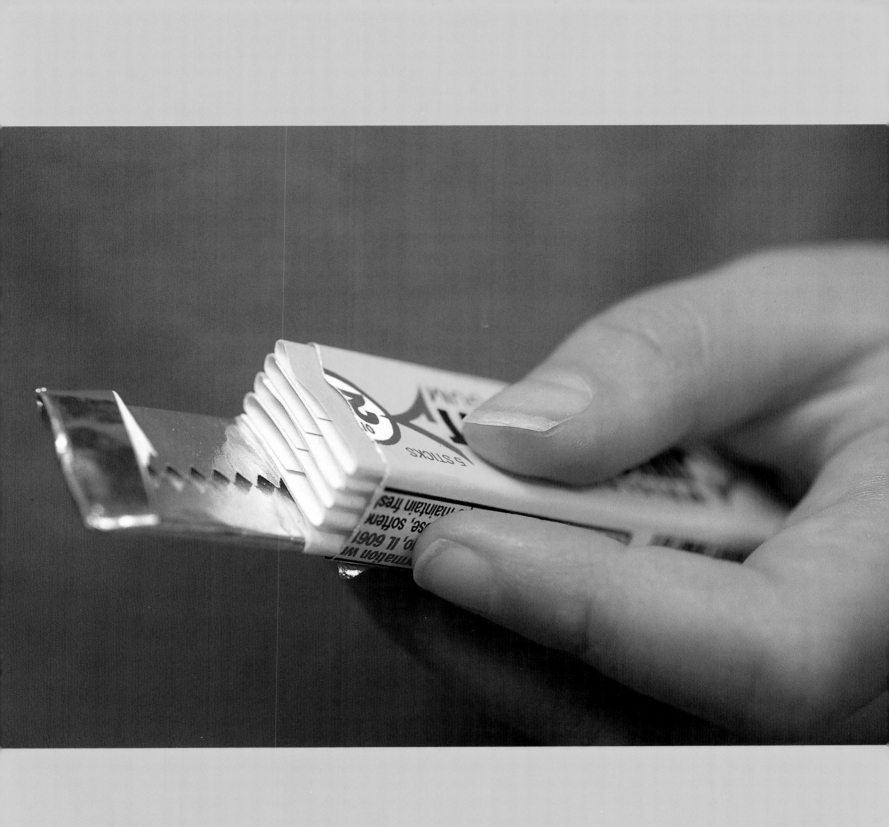

$$\frac{1}{4}$$

of a dollar

.25   25%

1796 - Tennessee - 2002

1803 - Ohio - 2002

1818 - Illinois - 2003

1819 - Alabama - 2003

$$\frac{1}{3}$$

of a traffic light

.33   33%

$$\frac{2}{3}$$

of a place setting

.66   66%

$$\frac{3}{4}$$

of a sandwich

.75   75%

$$\frac{99}{100}$$

of a dollar

.99   99%

1

whole pizza

1.00   100%

This is for my students at Fremont Open Plan, who inspired the idea.—SG

To my wife Kathy and daughters Kayla and Hannah—the fractions in my life that are far greater than the sum of the parts.—ST

TRICYCLE PRESS
a little division of Ten Speed Press
P.O. Box 7123
Berkeley, California 94707
www.tenspeed.com

Design by Catherine Jacobes
Typeset in Syntax

First Tricycle Press printing, 2003
Printed in Singapore

2 3 4 5 6 — 07 06 05 04

Library of Congress Cataloging-in-Publication Data

Gifford, Scott, 1955-
   Piece=part=portion : fractions=decimals=percents / by Scott Gifford ; photographs by Shmuel Thaler.
      p. cm.
Summary: Explains how in the language of mathematics, fractions,decimals and percents are three different ways of describing the same parts of things.
   ISBN 1-58246-102-3
   1. Fractions—Juvenile literature. 2. Logic, Symbolic and mathematical—Juvenile literature. [1. Fractions. 2. Decimal fractions. 3. Percentage.] I. Thaler, Shmuel, ill. II. Title.
   QA117.G54 2003
   513.2'6—dc21
                                                    2003006118